Elephant
LITTLE

First edition 2007

Copyright © 2007 Anno Domini Publishing
1 Churchgates, The Wilderness, Berkhamsted, Herts HP4 2UB
Text copyright © 2007 Catherine House
Illustrations copyright © 2007 Olwyn Whelan

Publishing Director Annette Reynolds
Editor Nicola Bull
Art Director Gerald Rogers
Pre-production Krystyna KowalskaHewitt
Production John Laister

ISBN: 978-1-59325-093-5

Published in 2007 in the US and Canada by The Word Among Us Press
9639 Doctor Perry Road Ijamsville, Maryland 21754
www.wordamongus.org
800-775-9673

Printed and bound in Singapore

LITTLE Elephant

by Catherine House and Olwyn Whelan

One sunny morning, Little Elephant was thinking.
He looked up at the sky. High above flew a large flock
of flamingos.

"Does God love the birds in the sky?" he asked.

"Yes, Little Elephant!" replied his mother. "God made all the birds
that fly in the sky, and he loves them very much."

Little Elephant kept thinking.

Little Elephant and his mother began to walk along the old elephant path.

"Be careful!" his mother warned him. "Always look to see where you are going."

At that moment, Little Elephant spotted something sleeping in the sun by the edge of the path.
It was a snake.

The snake slowly lifted his head.

He stared at the elephants for a moment and then disappeared into the long grass.

"Does God love snakes?" asked Little Elephant.

"Yes, Little Elephant!" replied his mother. "God made the creatures that crawl along the ground. Even snakes are part of God's wonderful world."

Little Elephant kept thinking.

The two elephants passed a hill of rocks and boulders.
Little Elephant stopped for a moment to look.
On top of a rock was a family of hyraxes
playing in the sun.
    "Does God love hyraxes?"

"Yes, Little Elephant!" replied his mother. "God made the animals that hide among the rocks, and he loves them very much."

Little Elephant kept thinking.

Later that morning, the two elephants came to the ocean. They stood on the edge of a cliff and looked out across the water. They watched as a family of whales swam into sight.

"Does God love the creatures that live in the ocean?" asked Little Elephant.

"Yes, Little Elephant!" replied his mother. "God made the fish and all the creatures that live in the sea, and he loves them very much."

Little Elephant kept thinking.

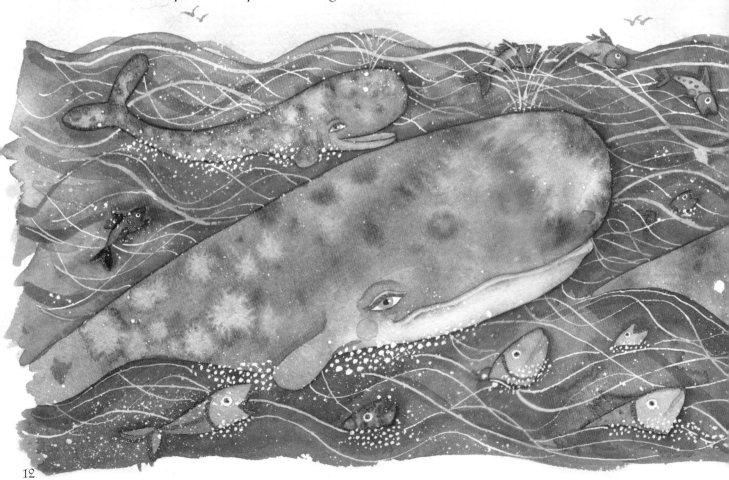

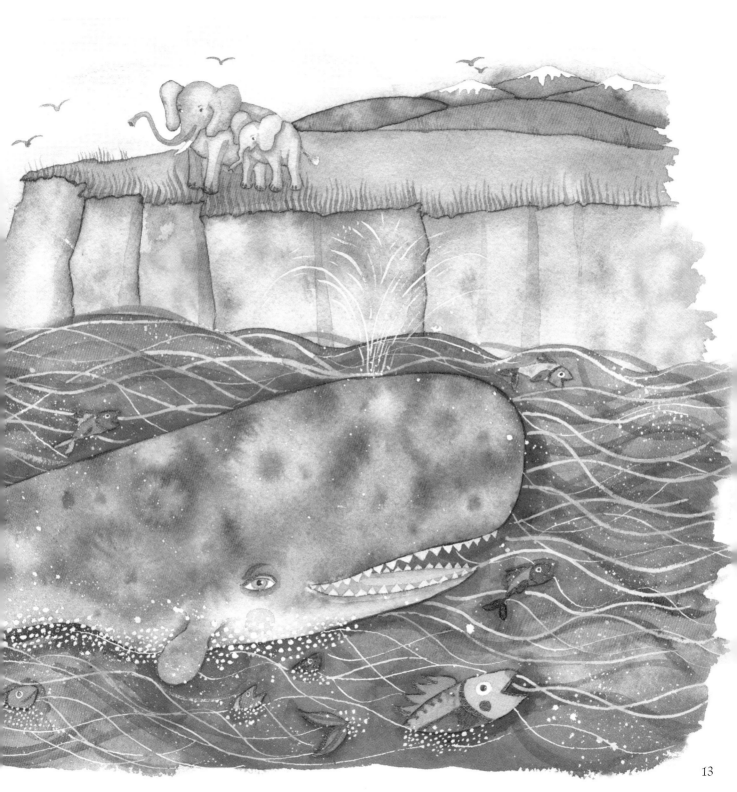

That afternoon, the elephants passed through a large, flat plain.
They stood and watched the animals grazing on the grass.
A herd of giraffes galloped past.
"Does God love the animals on the plains?" asked Little Elephant.

"Yes, Little Elephant!" replied his mother.
"God made all the animals that move along the ground,
and he loves them very much."

Little Elephant kept thinking.

It was now late in the day, but the sun was still bright and hot. Little Elephant began to feel tired. His mother found some shade under a spreading thorn tree.

Little Elephant looked up into the branches. A leopard was resting there. Her mouth was open wide, and the elephants could see her sharp, pointed teeth.

"Does God love leopards?" asked Little Elephant, as he quickly moved away.

"Yes, Little Elephant!" his mother replied as they walked away. "God made the leopards and all the animals that hunt, and he loves them very much."

Little Elephant kept thinking.

On their way home, the elephants walked past some tall termites' nests. Little Elephant put his trunk in one of the holes to see what it was like. Inside, the termites were busy as they worked to build their nest.

"Does God love insects?"

"Yes, Little Elephant!" came the reply. "God made the insects that wriggle and crawl and fly in the air and gave them all a job to do. He loves even the termites that are hidden away and out of sight."

Little Elephant kept thinking.

Down by the river, it was bath time. Little Elephant loved playing in the mud. Suddenly there was a splash nearby. Two round eyes were watching him silently from the water.

"Does God love crocodiles?" asked Little Elephant in a very low voice.

"Yes, Little Elephant!" replied his mother. "God made all the creatures that live in the water, and he loves them very much. But now it is time for us to go."

Little Elephant had so much to think about.

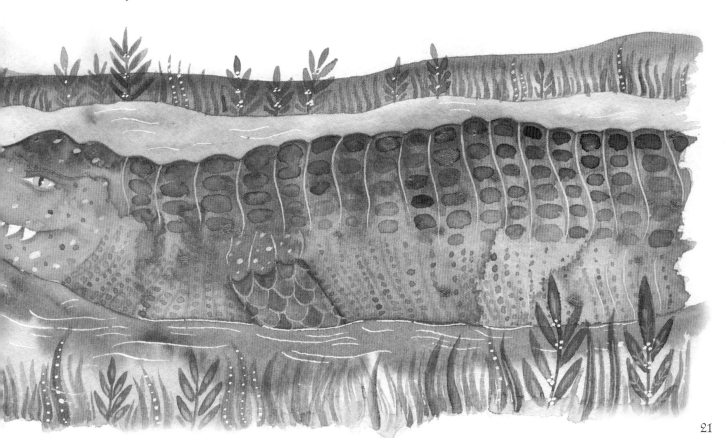

As the day came to an end, the two elephants joined the rest of the herd in the forest. The stars were beginning to come out, and Little Elephant could hear the call of the night birds through the trees. He always felt a little afraid as the sun disappeared from the sky.

Moving closer to his mother, Little Elephant had one last question to ask.

"Does God love me?"

"Yes, Little Elephant!" replied his mother. "God loves you very much. He loves you because he made you. He loves you because there is no other elephant quite like you and you are special to him."

"God's love will always be with you, Little Elephant," his mother continued. "When you are in the forest, God is there. When you walk across the plains, God will not leave you. If you cross the oceans, you will find that God's love will go with you."

Little Elephant was very tired. It had been a long day, and he had done a lot of thinking. Quietly, Little Elephant lay down beside his mother.

"Thank you, God, for loving all the creatures you have made," he whispered, as he closed his eyes. "Thank you, God, for loving me."